MW00906177

To all the women in my family who have shared their knowledge. To my grandmother Rose, my mother Maggie and my father Richard Wallingham — EM

For Sarah & Ginger — CW

Paperback edition published in Canada and the USA in 2010 by Groundwood Books

Groundwood Books / House of Anansi Press
110 Spadina Avenue, Suite 801, Toronto, Ontario M5V 2K4
or c/o Publishers Group West
1700 Fourth Street, Berkeley, CA 94710

We acknowledge for their financial support of our publishing program the Canada Council for the Arts, the Government of Canada through the Canada Book Fund (CBF) and the Ontario Arts Council.

Canada Council for the Arts
Conseil des Arts du Canada

Library and Archives Canada Cataloguing in Publication
McLeod, Elaine, 1955–
Lessons from Mother Earth / story by Elaine McLeod ;
pictures by Colleen Wood.
ISBN 978-0-88899-832-3
I. Wood, Colleen, 1958– II. Title.
PS8575.L4607L48 2010 jC813'.6 C2009-906512-6

Cover design by Alysia Shewchuk
Printed and bound in China

LESSONS *from* MOTHER EARTH

Story by ELAINE McLEOD
Pictures by COLLEEN WOOD

GROUNDWOOD BOOKS
HOUSE OF ANANSI PRESS
TORONTO BERKELEY

GRANDMA said, “Tess, are you hungry?”

“No,” I said.

Grandma said, “Tess, are you busy?”

“No,” I said.

“Well, then,” Grandma said, “let’s put on our boots and our sweaters. I am going to show you my garden.

"We must take a small knife. We must take a small bucket for you and my favorite old birchbark basket that my aunt Lucy left me. I will carry a paper bag just in case."

I had been visiting Grandma since I was born, five years ago, but I had never explored her garden.

We walked slowly along the trail behind Grandma's house. Grandma was looking down the banks and then up at the hills.

I asked her if she was lost, or if she really even had a garden.

Grandma pinched her lips and just ignored me.

We walked along for a while. Then she said, “Come on, Tess. We will go down the trail along the creek. You are just about old enough to learn the rules of the garden.

“Not everything in the garden is ready for picking just yet. Each little gift comes at its own special time. If everything came at the same time, we wouldn’t be able to collect it all.

"I was taught by my mother, your great-grandmother, about the plants. You must learn the rules, too. Tess, the number one rule is that you must always take good care of our garden."

As we walked, Grandma talked. "I was taught that if you take more plants than you need, they will never grow back. But if you don't pick any and just leave them sitting year after year, they will slowly wither away and die. To pick just enough is the secret.

"While you're picking, say a little prayer thanking Mother Earth for these beautiful gifts. Be careful, Tess, that you don't trample the bushes, especially the berry bushes. Once they are trampled and broken, they don't grow again.

"Tess, you must always take care of our garden. Never throw rubbish around. If you are careful and thankful, my granddaughter, our garden will care for you. There is plenty for everyone to share if we don't destroy the soil.

“I am old now but it has always cared for me. It has always cared for your mother and if you take care, I know this garden will also care for your children.

"Now," Grandma said, "we will pick some lamb's-quarters for supper and a few to freeze for winter. Just pinch them off above the ground and put them in your bucket. The cranberries and rosehips are not ready. They are waiting for their turn, after the raspberries and blueberries.

“Look over there, Tess. The dandelion shoots are ready. This is going to be a good year for the plants. You can tell by all the buds. Soon the mushrooms will be popping up in the field just beyond the trees. On this side of the hill the blueberries will nourish you for weeks as long as you care for the garden.”

Grandmother and I picked and picked. The sun shone down on us in the garden. I could hear Grandmother talking a little to herself, a little to me and a little to Mother Earth.

"Grandma, you sure have a big garden, and now I know where your garden is."

Grandma just pinched her lips and kept on picking.

I whispered, "Thank you, Mother Earth. Thank you for sharing. And mostly, Great Spirit, thank you for such a wise grandma."